CW01175594

The Hollow Traveller

Endings From a Dying Universe

J.L. Oakman

For the travellers, and those who wander with or without purpose.

For those who are lost, and those who have no desire to be found.

Endings

Poisonous

I have been to so many worlds, seen so many galaxies. I have seen skies of blue and gold, spined oceans of roiling madness, titanic steepled towers built for a purpose long since lost.

But I have never seen life.

I have encountered only endings, every story long since concluded; I have never seen a planet thriving. Is this it? Have all planets run their course? Are the conditions of the universe such that life can no longer prosper as once it did?

Perhaps, perhaps not. I am no scientist. I'm just a traveller, telling my story.

Let me tell you of one of the many worlds I have seen.

The only planet of a binary star system, its orbit was wide and eccentric. Having scanned the planet and found it surprisingly habitable, I landed by the most ancient of ruins I could find, and chose to wander my way around the world, tracing its history as best I could. It's a way to pass the time, when that is all you have.

This planet had borne various races of burrowing creatures. It seemed that life had evolved from the oceans to the underground, ignoring the dry surface entirely. I discovered ancient records telling of how poisonous the skin of this planet was, how vile and toxic the ground had become from some awful reaction in the atmosphere. I found no such toxins, but carried on with caution.

The first sentient civilisation built grand networks of caverns underground. The wiser they became, the further underground they fled, constantly fearing the poisons of the surface. It seems they were right to fear, too, for I discovered records that suggested the poison had begun to seep deeper into the soil, and those that still lived close to the surface died this way. It was in an especially deep tunnel, so close to the centre of the planet that these dark places were surprisingly warm, that I discovered a tunnel upward. Not a gentle incline, either, but a sharp ascent that brought me back to the surface far sooner than I had anticipated.

Here is where I discovered the next great civilisation of this planet's history. They had discovered a method of filtering the poison from the ground, sucking it away and ejecting it into firm, unyielding masses of gel they abandoned in the least habitable lands. In this way, the race found themselves as the first living beings on the surface of this planet, and soon they used their new technologies to spread across its skin. I found monumental cities that stretched across continents, and great rails that once carried trains between them.

I found the remnants of some third great people in a stony valley, far from the steel hives I had come to know before. Here, there were the derelict carcasses of brilliant ships, built to ride the skies. Their histories suggested that these ships had been built to escape the tyranny of those who governed the surface cities. A new civilisation was born in the clouds, once again exiled from the surface of their own planet.

I will admit that, when I discovered the reason for this sky-riding people's downfall, I wept. It seems whatever created this poison, the poison I could find no trace of, had continued to grow stronger. No longer could the surface cities keep up with this poison by pouring it into their valleys and gulches, so a new technology was created – instead of refining the poison into a safe ichor it was pumped directly into the sky. Poisonous clouds then littered the horizon, keeping the toxins away from the surface cities.

This, of course, was the end of the skyfolk. The people died, and their ships floated unmanned, for a while. The surface peoples saw this as a great success at first; their rebellious child had been silenced, and their poisons once again no longer threatened their civilisation. I cannot comprehend this; the parent civilisation killed its child, to buy itself a few more years.

Not even that, for it seems within one cycle around this planet's sun the end came for the second civilisation. The skyships began to break down and without the care of their owners they fell to the ground. Titanic vessels crashed down with such awful force that much of the surface of this planet was scorched, and all life upon the planet was ended.

Almost all life, I should say. For it seemed that the second civilisation was not the only race of people to escape their underground ancestral home. At the freezing poles of the world I found the ruins of another race; one that had evolved naturally to arrive at the surface of the planet. In those inhospitable frozen wastes they made their homes. These people were fascinated with the awful green sky above them; for they had never seen the stars or even their own sun, such was the damage the second civilisation had brought upon this world.

All records I could find suggest this race prospered for a great deal of time, millennia perhaps. They never dared venture beyond their icy homes, yet they were not unwise; for they knew they had been deprived of the sky. They feared the poisonous clouds that had been the end of all others, and their scientists worked to discover some ultimate solution to this toxic problem.

They found it, eventually. They found a way to completely nullify the poison and convert it into clean air and useable resources. They rolled out gigantic contraptions across their homes and activated them all, cleaning the skies and earth and air.

Air. Their air. Here, I believe, was the downfall of the final race of this planet.

You see, it had been too long. They had lived so long upon the surface they had evolved first to ignore the poison, and finally to rely upon it. It had been so subtle, so slow, that they had not noticed this change. Their dream of cleansing the atmosphere, of seeing their own twin stars, was their undoing. They cleaned the world of all its poisons, and destroyed themselves in the process.

And so there it was. A perfectly clean world, bearing so many histories upon and within its skin. I stayed on that world for centuries, absorbing their lives and past, but one day I had to move on. It is strange how detached you can become, when endings are all you are party to. That is my tale, my friend; shall I tell you another?

Mechanical

Shall I tell you another story, one of the many endings I've seen? Might as well, no? There is only time left now, I think.

A different one this time. Let me tell a story of a smog-drowned world of soot and steel, once a pivotal piece of a massive empire.

Yes, there were races and planets that grew up so close together that interplanetary, and eventually intergalactic, unions were formed. They never lasted long, but always burned brightly. This world I visited had been a part of one of the largest societies I've ever found, though few even knew of it in the grand scheme of things.

I was fascinated by what I found upon that planet. I was greeted by the still twitching limbs of long dead machines; massive arms and titanic hooks built for industry on an impossibly large scale.

Only one race ever achieved sentience on this planet. There were a few smaller scaled creatures, but I could only find the remnants of a single people that covered the surface. These peoples spread across the skin of the planet in tribes, and worshipped the stars and sky above them. Their star was a glowing, shifting mass of higher elements; it is not hard to imagine their worship.

Then, the overseers came. I am still unsure from where they originated; perhaps one of the many planets that entropy reached before me, forever erasing its history. They fell from the skies in mighty ships; and thus a race of sky worshippers found their gods.

From the few tribal records I could find, it seems the overseers rapidly subjugated these people. What began as excited worship quickly became indoctrination as the overseers set up monumental mining operations and gigantic networks of factories, putting the native race to work.

You see, this planet was extremely close to a remarkably hot star. The surface was scorched and rich in valuable minerals and exotic energies. It is a wonder life was able to flourish there at all! Thus, the scorched rock soon became a planetwide industrial operation, as entire continents were stripped bare of resources and then turned to factories, labour machines, and shipping networks used to transfer masses of resources offworld.

I have found no evidence in my travels that the natives of this rare and strange world ever left their home planet. These people who worshipped the stars sent their wealth up to them, but were never allowed to go themselves.

This planet became a vital pawn in the industrial complex of an empire that spanned galaxies. The wealth that poured from this small, burning rock had an impact across the stars, making the overseers rich and powerful.

It saddens me, how little of the native art I found. Once they were subjugated much of their history was destroyed, and they were forbidden from practicing their old ways. In the small hives they lived in, though, I did find some record of their fascinations. Their art was drawn across starmaps; beautiful sprawling canvasses, using their local star signs as inspiration. Not only their art though, for even their language used characters and words clearly once based on the night sky.

The art mutated over time, though. Newer hives could not successfully imitate the old designs, and soon I discovered why – mining, ore refinement, the constant transit of ships on- and offworld – it all produced smog. Within a century or two the sky was entirely lost; hidden behind a veil of black and grey soot.

I think this may have been the tipping point, though I cannot be certain. The race found some record of its history, or perhaps rediscovered its fascination with the sky, and could stand their subjugation no longer. They turned the tools of their masters against them and slew the overseers that inhabited their world.

I expect it may have helped that, by this time, the empire the overseers ruled had crumbled, and this planet was long abandoned. Retribution did not come; or perhaps it was simply pre-designed.

The smog cleared, the people regained their sky – but the planet was ruined. Long gone were the old creatures and flora, and all the landscape was permanently tarnished by newly redundant machinery. The people slowly reclaimed their old identity, or built a new one based on the old, but never did they feel the success they once had.

The race died out, insignificant but free. At least they had their stars.

Resurgent

How many stars do you think we can see from here, my friend? Fewer than I wish, and certainly fewer than there should be; but they cannot sustain themselves indefinitely. Nor can any race, of course; every race has an ending, and all bar mine have long since been reached now.

There was an interesting planet though; one that seemed almost unwilling to give up supporting life upon its skin. It was a small world, in a system with no other planets, and just a dull yellow star to orbit around. Yet, it had been within the habitable zone of the star, and had certainly supported life.

This world held two major continents, with a smattering of small islands dotted about the vast ocean. On one continent, I found the first race; a pioneering people, driven by exploration and a need to discover. Everywhere I went I found simple, utilitarian structures; storehouses, dwellings, workshops, and little else; but every so often I found huge towers, relics of their need to see the land. These towers were beautifully crafted; furnished with all sorts of unnecessary detail and adornment. These towers were clearly extremely important to the race; and in fact I found what I believe to have been mentions of offerings and sacrifices made to them. Perhaps the very concept of discovery was like a god to these people; or maybe I'm making undue assumptions, but either way these towers were of extreme importance to this race.

They spent a long time on this one massive continent, developing ever-more advanced cultures, each always certain the ocean stretched on forever. They were entirely unaware that across the vast ocean there was a twin island, abundant with flora and resources, and unclaimed by intelligent life.

For such an exploratory people, it took them a long time to decide to sail. It wasn't until they were capable of basic flight, and they discovered some of the smaller islands proving they were not completely alone, that they decided to dedicate their time and resourcefulness to ship-craft. They did, though, and I found a great deal of evidence suggesting that they set sail, discovered the other island, and a twin empire was established. I found histories of trade, and discourse, and change; never war though, these people had no interest in war.

They did eventually die out, though, as all do. It seems their death was consumption and reliance on their limited land; they were not prepared for blights to ravage their food stores. With all the world charted and under their control, their ability to explore could do them no good, and the land was the death of them.

On the other continent, there was no evidence of the other half of this great empire; all

I learned, I learned from the land I had first landed on. Why? Well, on the other continent, another race had laid new ruins over the top of the first.

This second civilisation confused me greatly. It looked as though one civilisation died and then, aeons later, another rose up – it appeared that one did not evolve from the other.

Beyond that, they were morphologically entirely distinct from each other; they had no common origin at all. So where had this second race come from? The clearest answer was just a second rising species, but something still seemed off – this second race was so different, so poorly matched to the genetic diversity of the first, I knew there was a stranger answer. Or, perhaps, I have simply told myself later that I knew in advance what was coming. I am uncertain.

The answer was buried deep under a landlocked river in the second continent. There, I found evidence of a devastating crash; a ship from another world had struck the planet, and the crew had died where they fell. The ship landed in the river, and the crew's corpses mouldered and festered until the running water eventually broke down the exterior of the ship, and flooded in to where the bodies lay. This rotten detritus was carried by the river out to a massive lake, where various rivers replenished the rich silt, and kept a constant, yet gentle, underwater tumult.

With these unlikely, perfect conditions, the near impossible occurred, and alien bacteria found a suitable new home. Over time, these thriving bacteria evolved and changed to better fit their environment, and then to grow within it. From this lake sprung forth a new race, thoroughly distinct both from the other race of this world, and from the race of other beings from which they had been seeded.

This race developed less; a primitive society stretching across the skin of the second continent but never daring to venture out into the boundless sea. These people worshipped the sun, and allowed it to inform their art and their limited language: collections of stonework inscriptions and simple paintings could be found all across the continent.

These people were not given the time to develop beyond this stage. From their unlikely beginnings, they met an all too common end: a massive ball of stone and ice fell through their atmosphere and stuck the land, burning almost all away in moments. The few who survived were frozen in the dust storm ice-age that followed.

Three distinct races influenced the civilisation of this world, before eventually falling to circumstances they were never prepared for or aware of. Too often is this the case, my friend; so many have met their end due to wild and unpredictable influence from the unknown.

We have much time to pass, would you care for another story?

Silent

I have more stories, if you'd like to pass some time? I have so many stories of my travels; from a time when such travels were possible. I visited so many dead planets; saw the remnants of so many long dead empires. It is still my belief that, by the time I was travelling the universe, some fundamental law of nature had changed, and the conditions of the universe would no longer support life. In my many millennia travelling the cosmos, not once have I found even the faintest signs of a still-living thing. I am not one to make assumptions based on incomplete understanding, my friend, but it is my belief that this universe has passed. It is dead, and we are merely the last bystanders at its burial.

I was meandering my way through a remarkably old system. Three planets orbited a cold, dead star; a barren orb of used fuel, casting no further light upon its captive worlds. Two of the planets had clearly held no life; one was a giant stone, trapped at the very edge of this star's gravity; the other had once been a flourishing jungle; tall poles, with bark of pure silver, with no minds to ever appreciate the twinkling as light bounced between trees in the dense forest.

At first I presumed the third, the closest to the star, was as barren as the first. It bore none of the typical signs of life; there were no structures, no bones, and most tragically, no art. Something, however, seemed wrong with what my scans told me, so I set down upon that planet and began my slow, ponderous investigation.

It was a desert planet. A single, impossibly large desert that stretched across the surface of the world. I wandered, exploring the sands and searching for variance, for a while. The winds around the planet were consistent and slow; a constant, gentle breeze altering the landscape over the span of centuries. This led to dunes like mountain ranges; ever grander peaks dominating the skyline with each I summited. These mountains of sand were nomads; across hundreds of years the gentle winds made them appear to wander, a single mountain range slowly rolling across the world. Of course, the individual grains of sand that made up each mountain were constantly changing; but at such a small scale, those mountains were invisible anyway.

It is in these grains of sand I found the civilisation of this world. There I found the bones, the structures, the legacy of this silent desert. At least, I found whispers of its ending. Here more than most so much of the history was lost to me; so much culture wiped out to all future wanderers.

I can only guess at the true nature of this society; and you know only too well that I am no scientist, just a traveller. But I suppose there is no-one else to make more educated guesses, so mine is the only story this universe will hear.

I imagine it was once a thriving planet, with a typical evolutionary past; land-dwelling folk that once crawled from the sea. With industrial discovery came pollution, and a cycle of warming that caused the ocean to swell as the ice caps diminished. Yes, there was water on this world, once. There still was when I wandered it, in a sense.

Why did this culture crave energy so? Given the desperate measures they went to, their need must have been great indeed. I believe, from what small hints at their existence I found, that the seeds of environmentalism I found on so many planets never took root here. The ideology, perhaps, was simple; anything that could be used to fuel their ever-growing lust for energy would be. I imagine great plants built to burn minerals, and cells fuelled by radioactive isotopes. I cannot know this, of course, but at least that would help understand the lengths they then went to.

A technology was devised. One unlike anything I had, or have, encountered anywhere else. Cold fusion on a miniature scale; free energy for life. Tiny machines were built and released into the wild, which would collect the nearest atoms and molecules and burn them into nothingness, capturing every speck of energy their matter contained.

I may not be a scientist, but I do know the energy contained within matter. I have seen weapons of destruction capable of turning infinitesimally small fragments of matter into utter annihilation. The energy contained within a single atom is unfathomable.

But it wasn't enough, not for these people. What engine did they so desperately need to power, that they unlocked the very power of the universe and found it wanting? More and more of these machines were created, to harvest ever more of the energy of their world.

The process of this fusion produced a queer byproduct; impossibly small grains of silt: the ashes of burnt atoms. That was the desert I trod. I cannot imagine how great and full this planet must once have been, to produce deserts of such fine ash.

I do not know why, or how, the tiny machines were turned against their masters. Was it an accident of design; the people unable or unwilling to imagine their own creations turning against them? An act of suicidal terrorism? The awful realisation that such machines could be used for military purposes, and that across imaginary lines in the ground was a lush garden of awaiting fuel? I cannot know, nor do I think I wish to. For whatever reasons, this species consumed itself, and its very planet with it. Eventually, these machines buried their planet in useless ash, and set upon themselves. Where was this last energy released? Perhaps it would explain the strange winds of this world, or the warmth of the ashen desert. In honesty, this is just another aspect of that world I can never truly understand.

I left that planet with a greater haste than perhaps was necessary. I do not like to consider the people of that planet, nor the unquenchable desires that lead to their demise. But there it is; the tale of the silent planet. Would you like another?

Grand

Look out, there; do you see the last few gleaming stars? I have visited many of them; most are dead and barren. Some will have gone cold by now, their light some final spectre of resistance against the dark.

Sorry. It has grown ever harder not to drown in the impossibility of our situation; the sheer emptiness of the sky above. How long do you think it will be, before the last sparks are dimmed?

Well. We still have time. Plenty, I'd expect. Shall I tell you another story? Perhaps a more positive one, this time; we have become quite dour in our stagnation.

I was in a small system; its galaxy devastated by a recent encounter with a far larger cloud. Two planets orbited a shining white star in erratic chaos. One of the planets was, I believe, once a moon of some other planet. It was built of endless collisions leaving their detritus upon a growing shore; but it bore no life at all.

The other was a huge, grey orb. While not significantly larger than many planets I have visited, this one was unusually dense. Scans indicated the entire core was a molten plasma of super-heavy compounds, with a dense metal crust that stretched for miles. The gravity of this planet was immense; so great I imagine with just a little assistance it could have become some minor star in its own right. A curiosity; but I have seen countless curiosities in my time. I would have abandoned this odd metal ball of a planet had it not borne the one thing I am truly fascinated by; a history. This planet had once held life.

Walking along its surface, I saw no evidence of this. The skin of this planet was flat and gentle; sheer gravity holding back any great mountains or valleys. From the surface, I could see to the horizon in all directions; a great, unchanging wave of dull golden brown.

I was confused, to say the least. I wandered the surface for a long while seeing no signs of life at all. No structures, no marking, no art of any kind. I thought that perhaps my poor ship had finally failed me, and that the scans were wrong. I returned to the ship to repeat the tests, intending to leave as soon as I had confirmed my fears.

But the scans repeatedly came back positive. There had been life upon this planet, and it still bore the markers of their history. I had seen many a planet before that had annihilated itself and the surface of its planet; but never so cleanly. I delved deep into the answers my scans provided, trying to find what was so well hidden from me.

It was obvious, really. I should have understood within minutes of landing. The entire surface of the planet was littered with the remnants of a truly mighty civilisation; just on a slightly different scale to what I had expected. The rest of my investigation had to be conducted from afar, but I discovered a civilisation that had once been grander than most.

This planet's gravity had been far too strong for large life to prosper; but as I have found, life tends to find a way anyway. Instead of growing large and then growing complex, the life of this planet simply developed complexity without size. Microscopic organisms, compressed collections of impossibly efficient cells working in perfect unison; intelligent life, the size of most microbes.

They developed tools and architecture to match their size; tiny cities like patches of mould across the surface of the world. Their architectural style was efficient; almost like a computer. Complex grids and lattices of structures; building tall against their aggressive gravity.

I did discover their art; such as it was. They did not paint, or craft like most. Instead, their art was life itself; they grew shifting masses of bioluminescent cells, patches of evershifting colour and orbs that would glow in the night.

It seemed that this people had never developed war; or perhaps they simply grew past it. For their entire planet held a single, unbroken layer of their history. Cities, gardens, and forests in minute scale spread across the entire world, with no borders or segregations of any kind. And then there was their ending.

Every population has an ending. A final passing from thriving civilisation to broken ruins. This planet was no different; this race had died out aeons ago; but it's ending was a little calmer than most. There was no great war, no scientific mishap, no overreaching for wealth or resources. As the sun grew hotter the world became less hospitable, and the population naturally declined. In time, the hardiest looked out upon their dying world and realised their time upon its surface was coming to an end, and thus came together. The city across the skin of the world grew dormant, with small pockets of surviving life lasting out. The heat grew, and slowly these communities grew smaller and weaker, before each eventually breathed their last.

They never struggled against their fate. They held their last, and held it well, producing beauty and art to the end; but eventually death came to the last of their kind, and it was welcomed without mourning. This race, born impossibly, grew grand and prosperous, and eventually faded to nothingness with but a gentle, smiling sigh. I have never seen a people quite like them.

Origin

I'm sorry I've not been especially optimistic recently. It's hard, you know? Look out, into that emptiness beyond, into those last few stars I'll never see. I like to imagine one of them, somewhere, holds a thriving civilisation just starting to explore the boundless infinity open to it. Discovering wonders, considering new ideas, creating art.

But I know there is no such people. The sky holds just dying stars, burnt out worlds, and us now. Just us. Would you like another story? I've plenty left to tell. I know of a planet where, every morning, the three moons would-

Or perhaps you'd like to hear my story. Just perhaps.

It's not very interesting, are you sure? OK, I'll tell you my story. But first, a warning; none of what I am about to tell you is true. You'll understand soon.

I am the last surviving member of a proud civilisation. We valued knowledge and discovery above all else; a culture that never grew past its frontier roots. I was born and grew up on the moon of our home planet. It was beautiful; a verdant satellite full of twisting trees that would wander across the grand plains in the wind. Ever above me was our homeworld; a glittering beacon of light illuminating my side of the moon. Two other planets drifted lazily in the sky around our little sun; both were colonised generations before my birth, and my family took me to holiday on the furthest planet, a ball of free-flowing ice, after I graduated flight school.

Years went by as I progressed in my career as a pilot for the finest planet-faring ships we had at our disposal. Then, one day, I was selected to take part in a test program. A new ship had been created, and it was ready for a live flight. This ship, quickly labelled the grand flagship of our people, was the first of its kind, capable of bridging the gap between stars. I never fully understood the science, but the simple explanation was that the ship would slip across possibilities and into a wormhole, and out again by its target in the blink of any eye. Faster than light travel; the impossible dream was realised.

But on my very first flight something went wrong. Oh, my ship was perfectly fine, and there I was orbiting an alien star; but my ship had gone haywire. It ardently refused to accept my homeworld still existed. I could see it through my instruments, but my ship assured me that I was looking at empty space. So it never allowed me to plot a route back; for this ship could only find its way to stars, where warmth and light would charge its thirsty cells. And thus that was my fate; travelling the stars alone, sending all my findings home, but never able to return.

A sad story, yes? But filled with that little hope of finding great new things, and the knowledge I would forever be helping my people.

Yes. It would be nice, if it were true. But, as I said, that was a lie. Allow me to explain.

Those are the memories I woke with, millennia ago. My eyes opened and, as I lay in the dark, I briefly believed them. But then dawn struck me; a red light from a softly burning alien star, and I knew those memories were hollow. As I replayed those memories in my mind it did not feel as though I had experienced them; rather, it was like a video feed of a life, played back behind my eyes for an audience of one. But they were not memories – I did not feel emotions associated with that I was supposedly recalling, I could not recount the taste of a single item I had consumed, nor the feel of any object I had touched.

My ship was real though. A ship capable of travelling the stars, if significantly more slowly than my false memories suggested. It took me very little time, relatively speaking, to understand what had happened. Allow me, dearest friend, to tell you the honest story of my world, and of my hollow return.

The previous location was in my ship's logs; the only co-ordinates it knew, apart from where I had woken up. I think they had assumed my belief that return was impossible would prevent me; for the ship held no such restrictions. My home planet orbited the closest star, a mere three light years away. It took a little less than eight 10thousand years to arrive, by my ship's understanding of the term "year". My people did not believe in the value of individual life so much as cultural memory; that those who sent me into space would never know my findings meant nothing, they cared only that some generation would benefit.

When I arrived, I learned that the image of my home in my mind was accurate, in part. My home planet was a disappointingly mundane world; a city-planet, not unlike hundreds I have visited since. Its only habitable moon was large, but it was no civilised world; by my reckoning it had been a military base.

Oh, I didn't mention; there was not a single living being present when I arrived. I did tell you, did I not, that I have never met a living being beyond myself? I meant that quite honestly.

The other planets in the system held some small influence of my people. The planet closest to the sun was scorched and dusty, but there I found small farming and mining settlements, once protected by long-collapsed domes. The further planet was truly beautiful, though held barely any remnants of my people. The planet was entirely covered in frozen water, but the core was an extremely dense soup of metals, making the gravity extraordinary. This, combined with constant magnetic storms at the poles, meant the ice was a constant tumult of massive shards, flowing like water. My people had set up orbiting research vessels, but almost all had been unmanned. Some still floated in the sky; drifting reminders of my people's dauntless curiosity.

I visited my homeworld last. There was very little left, but I have no great story to weave for you, either. A scorched husk; like so many others, my home planet had fallen to bickering, and burnt itself away entirely.

The moon is where I found my answers; though I had guessed most of them already, as I imagine you have in your own way. Like I said, the moon held military installations; from my investigation it seems likely that it is from there the weapons that ended my people were fired. I also found my home.

No small house that overlooked the glittering beacon of my homeworld though, absolutely not. My home was an engineering complex, and a cold metal slab.

You understand, don't you? It is there I was built, and there I was given false memories to incentivise my exploration of the stars. I believe they really were naturally curious about their frontiers, and that that is why they sent me on my way, and eagerly awaited any data I would send home to their descendants; but in the meantime, they consumed themselves with war.

I struggle to understand how they did not foresee me questioning my own nature. The memories they gave me told me to sleep once I had plotted a course, and once I awoke I would be at my destination; but with no reason to follow my memories, I instead just watched the centuries of flight roll by. Did they not expect me to question how so much time had passed between the start of journey and my arrival? Further, how did they expect me to reconcile my ability to walk on the heaviest and most aggressive of worlds, when the memories of my people tell of flimsy forms, used to low gravity and predator-free lands?

Perhaps they thought me incapable of questioning. Perhaps they did not see me as life at all; but just another lifeless drone sent out into the infinity beyond to further their understanding. I cannot say for certain, and I don't care to either. I have had plenty of time travelling the skies to ponder my own existence, and I daresay I know myself better than they did.

So there it is, my friend; the story of my people, and my origin. The story of the last life to be born, and to wander the universe.

My own people were not nearly so fascinating as many of the histories I have discovered. Shall I tell you of better places?

Multitudes

Would you care to hear of one my stranger findings? Of a journey that took me far from any planet, and almost ended my wandering?

As I have explained, my ship is designed only to visit still burning stars, to fuel its hungry cells. Well once, I detected something so very strange, so unlike anything I had encountered before, I had to investigate, even though it was far from the light of any sun. To convince my ship to travel this perilous voyage, I instead targeted a star far further than where I intended to go, but on the same path, and settled in. I rejected the long sleep, and watched intently as the centuries ticked by, until I approached the entity causing these strange readings. I forced my ship to shut down by ripping out its power cells; madness, perhaps, but I had to know.

I carefully guided it to a stop with the tools and power I had available, and ventured from my ship to investigate. Whatever this thing was, it was truly massive; thrice the size of most planets I have encountered, but not nearly as dense. As I approached, I still didn't understand what lay before me; it took some research before that became clear.

In my vision was a massive field of grey detritus, all patches of the same huge layer of material. On close inspection, this strange matter was dusty, crumbling to nothing in my hands, each particle drifting listlessly from me into space. Where I encountered it, this material was very thin, and overstretched. Elsewhere it was thick; such that I couldn't even breach the other side. This curious material stretched almost entirely around the non-planet like a skin; and that is precisely what I learned this thing was; this was the skin of some mighty behemoth; a truly massive entity that had somehow found itself alone in the depths of empty space.

I am not sure, however, that this was ever a single creature. I believe it was a colony of sorts, a mass of microscopic creatures congealed into the approximate shape of larger life. I have encountered many examples of such life on worlds I have visited; but even the largest corpses of these colonies were found within the oceans of appropriately sized worlds; never planetary in size.

Inside was more fascinating still; within the skin of this world-leviathan I found innumerable different races of what appeared to be aquatic life. I am unsure if any were every sentient; I certainly found markers of tribal natures and pack instincts, but whether they were capable of forming complex societies or producing art is beyond my knowledge.

So, what was this thing I had found? I believe the colony formed first. Perhaps even as some lifeform used to atmosphere somehow thrust into space and capable of surviving?

Perhaps that is too far-fetched, even for my own musings. Rather, I think it must have somehow evolved in space to begin with, most likely in a far more bountiful region at first, an asteroid belt maybe. For whatever reason, this example of its species, the only one I have ever found, grew to colossal proportions, and fostered its own ecosystem within its skin. While it still lived, I expect its skin was supple and giving, perhaps even allowing asteroids of ice to fill its core and supply it with fresh material. However it functioned, as it grew so did the life inside it, and over any number of millennia the races it bore grew complex and lively.

As all things do, this behemoth eventually passed. I was unable to find the reasons for its demise in my limited time there; age, an impact with something larger than it could cope with, or perhaps a mistake of one of the internal races; one way or another this great creature met its end. I cannot imagine how the internal environment changed as it rotted and collapsed, but it seems plausible that the lives inside were able to survive for some time after the death of their host. But without the organic repair of its skin, eventually this creature ruptured, and the creatures used to the comfortable embrace of this titan suddenly found themselves exposed to harsh space, and unsurprisingly this massive ecosystem met its end.

My ship groaned and shuddered when I restored its power. It was confused, uncertain as to why its momentum had been ripped away, and I felt the internal mechanisms of the ship scream as they tried to re-assert their previous heading. Pistons fired and valves burst; and I feared for a moment I would meet the same fate as the inhabitants of the leviathan, cast into empty space to drift aimlessly. But slowly my ship settled, and soon it was back on course to the far world I had told it to navigate to.

I cannot be sure, but that may have been the first time I truly feared for my life. That may just be because I am a hardy thing, unlikely to die in most circumstances, or maybe that is the first time I realised that not all life is born the same way, to the same style of planet, and that is the first time I considered myself truly alive.

Conjecture. Memories are fallible and easy to misplace or misinterpret. Another ending, my friend?

Still

Another story then, of another world's end? Have no fear, I've more memories of endings than there is time left to tell them.

Now, almost all planets I visited held, as you might expect, only the hollow bones of their races and cultures. Over the eons since life had thrived on each world, time and entropy had dragged them slowly back to dust and ruin. Allow me to tell you the story of an incredibly tranquil world, still firmly holding the remnants of its final breath.

This world had once resided in a binary star system, spinning precariously between its two stars. As the system danced around it, it floated motionless, drawn equally to the two massive bodies of fusion and fire.

How this little planet achieved its curious position I've no idea, but it remained there for a long time, spinning softly. Its unique situation caused a number of curiosities on the world; for one, this was a place that had never known night, as the entire surface of the planet was always bathed in burning light. The skin of the world was permanently baked, and yet somehow life grew on the surface.

These odd creatures were undoubtedly among the stranger of those I've encountered. They were a silicate based life form, looking much like the stone and earth around them. Much of one of these creature's bodies was contained in a large orb of rock atop two powerful legs; I believe there may have been some more complex organic material within these orbs, but by the time I found them any traces of such things were long gone.

They had no use for eyes, or any other typical sensory tool, for their world was constantly bathed in energy across much of the commonly visible spectrum. Instead, they had a powerful yet narrow third limb that I believe they used to tap on the ground, building a picture of the landscape through vibration. Just a theory, of course, I had no opportunity to ask the people themselves!

Their art was magnificent, and quite unique. This race appeared to have little or no concept of aging; they definitely suffered death, as do all living things, but they never succumbed to time as most do. So, rather than building anything of the scorched rock of the world, they used themselves as their canvas. Masses of these creatures would come together and lock their limbs into intricate, towering configurations, and remain there for as long as they so desired.

For whose purpose, given there were no eyes to appreciate them, I do not know. Perhaps these configurations were just pleasing to the participants, or perhaps the strange senses this race possessed were more sophisticated than I imagined.

But the end comes to all things, even this docile, stony race. I'm unsure what caused it, but something great interrupted the gravitational equilibrium this planet enjoyed, and it was flung far. Through some stroke of chance, these people were not simply plunged into one of their suns, doomed to be fuel for fusion, but instead their planet escaped the gravity of both entirely, and was sent on its own drifting journey away from warmth.

I assume it was the heat that they needed; but given their strange evolutionary path, I could easily be mistaken. One way or another, it was the stars that kept these people alive, as so often is the case, and without them they soon died.

Walking through this quiet planet, I was struck by how quickly the end must have come; some were still locked in their beautiful patterns, and countless other were dotted along the landscape, calm and still. Over time some had collapsed to sombre piles of stone, but largely this entire planet was almost precisely how I imagine it must have been in their last moments of warmth; barring the activity of life. A snapshot of life: motionless, but true.

I spent a long time there. It is rare I can stare at a once-living being directly; at a thing that had once thought and moved. I learned less of them than I wish I could have; they were simply so alien to my understanding, they were hard to comprehend fully. Nevertheless, I am glad I had the chance the find this cold, unchanging planet, that still held the closest remnants of life.

Not a happy tale, but an optimistic one, perhaps. I hope, and yes, I am capable of hope, that one day that planet finds its way to another warm star, and some aspect of what they were can return. This seems unlikely, given the state of the sky, but permit me my dreaming, my friend.

I'll be back in a moment, dear companion; but let me leave you with something I encountered a long time ago, perhaps it will keep you occupied.

Burn

The world ended four months ago.

You wouldn't know it for looking. Walk into the streets of my district where I write this and you'll see children playing, people ambling to work with briefcases in hand, dogs being walked by carefree owners. But like I said, the world has already ended, and these people are all dead. So am I, by the way, I'm no different to anyone else here.

The thing is, the end came to Cassiopeia II slowly. So slowly, most of us haven't even been touched by it yet. We will, that's for sure, but not yet.

Maybe I should explain. Cassiopeia II is the last surviving world of my people. A world that shines like a diamond when seen from the stars; our world was the home of our species, or so say the historians. Once our people began to dance among the stars, this planet of ours became a shining city of culture and enterprise.

A planet, or a city, I hope you ask. If I could see you, dear reader, I'd smile as I told you that our planet, the last gleaming bastion of our kind, is a single, impossibly large city. Long gone were the days of war and poverty, and so we looked to industry to answer all our wants. Our planet is a single forest of towering skyscrapers and metal monuments to our progress. A single mechanical heart, beating for our once-empire.

But then war found us once again. No outer race came to end us; no, we have never met another race of minds quite like ours, in all our explorations. No, be it jealousy, want, or change; our colony planets splintered endlessly into smaller and smaller factions. We watched in dismay as all our children across the stars erased themselves in fruitless wars. We were so sure we were safe. We were always so far ahead of them; our defences were impenetrable, against direct attacks, at least.

There lies our end, dear reader. In an unlikely innovation, our ruin was found. One of the last surviving colonies invented a chemical substance; an unstoppable reaction. The masses called it digital fire, and it's not hard to see why; once this chemical touches against any metal it ignites into beautiful blue tongues of unbearably hot fire. This fire does not seek wood, or other organic fuel sources; no, digital fire catches along all metals, and it is spreading itself across our shining city-world.

As the fire burns, it releases tiny spores; packets of that same base chemical, ready to catch against other metals. Our child colonies needed only sneak a few such spores onto a world; the unending reaction has done the rest.

They tried so many ways to stop it, at first. Water quenches the fire, but leaves the spores unharmed. As soon as it dries, the metal reignites. They discussed blasting away strips of our world, to leave segments unharmed; but these spores are light and are carried hither and thither with the wind. Should we have decided to burn away massive stretches of our own home we would have given ourselves days, if that.

So our world is aflame. A wildfire that cannot be stopped, controlled, or contained. At least a quarter of our world has burned away to pockmarked slag and bare dirt now. Dirt; I've never seen the stuff in its natural home. My life has been steel walls and shining floors.

The digital fire is accelerating; burning faster as more material makes itself available, and more spores are released. They estimate it will be a few months at most before all is consumed. This thin façade of normalcy will fade long before then.

I do so hope someone, one day, is able to read this. My own kind never will; our politicians turned our grand weapons toward our last splinter children and burned them away in monstrous retaliation; we are the last of our kind. I have no doubt that my species is ended. I refuse to believe we are unique though; I refuse to believe it is impossible for other minds to prosper.

I am a geneticist. My name is not important, and I have no desire to be remembered anyway. I just hope someone is able to read this; so my people may live on in memory. Perhaps we don't deserve even that honour; but I can't help but try. Written in the simplest of languages available to me, the structure of the most common atoms, I have encoded the story of my people's end, our last story, into the genetic code of one of the hardiest trees I have ever known. This story will be written into hundreds of seeds, waiting for fertile soil.

There is earth beneath the metal and stone of our world; I will never feel it, but perhaps these seeds can. I'm going to throw them to the wind; high into the air, where they may fly and scatter along the burning air currents until the last fires go out and our planet cools.

I cannot harbour the idea that our planet will lie lifeless forever. That we, the smartest beings known, were foolish enough to end all life in our petty struggles. Perhaps; with the seeds of life and enough time, some new intelligent thing will come to be. Perhaps, one day, they will find my story.

Lost

Sorry to be away so long, my friend; what did you think? The story of an ending, told by one who witnessed it, I found hidden within petrified wood. That world was an ancient forest planet when I found it; born, I believe, of those sturdy seeds. What wonders we can achieve, when it is not ourselves we fight for.

So, do you think we have time for more stories? It's getting awfully cold.

Alright. Allow me to tell you about a curious little society I discovered a long time ago, soon after my own journey had begun.

There were but two planets orbiting a cool yellow star. One was close; a burnt rock just barely holding onto its orbit; but the other was cool and stable.

The trouble was, this planet was in the midst of an awfully dense asteroid belt. I imagine this is what catalysed life on the planet to begin with; bombardment from the skies. Every few weeks on the planet a stone would rip through the atmosphere, giving the entire planet an edge of turmoil and unpredictability. I quite enjoyed it.

From what I can tell, life had grown up and prospered within the calmer cave networks on the planet. These cool crevices and tunnels would offer some relief from the bombardment, or at least give living things a better chance.

Sadly, by the time I arrived a far larger asteroid, a rogue moon I think, had collided with the planet. There was no respite to be had from such an impact; over half the world was burnt away in moments, and the other half burnt or froze in the firestorms and dust-cloud induced ice-age that followed. I could find very little of their civilisation at all; except that it had once been there. All had been scorched away.

That would have been the end of this sorry endeavour, had there not been a moon to this planet. There, I found the remnants of those who had escaped to a more stable home. You see, this moon was small, and not especially dense. As it was so near such a large planet, the moon was very rarely struck, and thus remained a safe haven for a very long time.

A great civilisation thrived for quite some time. They built high and wide across the moon, taking advantage of the low gravity for some truly wondrous architecture. One particular city, I recall, had developed a fashion for spiralling tower blocks that reached high into the air, intertwining or connecting at the top. They were easily capable of sending mining missions to their home planet, and so they rarely wanted for resources. From some limited records I could find, at one point they even set up farming operations in the cave networks of the planet, though this was unpredictably risky, and generally unpopular.

Their art was curious; unlike many I have seen, but unmistakable for its creative purpose. The most common artistic methods I found all referred to using a curious, ashen material as a medium; sculptures formed of this strange ash, or paints mixed with it. If what I found is to be believed, this ash was radioactive, though apparently not remotely harmful to the people who had evolved around it. This ash would begin to decay into nothing within a year, burning itself up across months. A sculpture would crumble to nothing, a painting would fade to just its canvas. I did not get to see any of their art first hand; so I am thankful they kept records of their methods and styles. This race, who could never feel entirely secure on their homeworld, had a curious fascination with transience; or perhaps I am looking too deeply into their inspirations.

So, as always, we approach the ending of this displaced civilisation. Overpopulation was their doom in the end; with such limited space, eventually a single grand city rolled across the entire moon, and when an incurable plague began to spread, there was nothing to be done.

This was not the end though, not yet; I have seen so many great empires fall to disease; but this one was different. In a last ditch attempt to save themselves, they created a small ship, to be sent out of the reach of their own star. They were not capable of sending large, manned missions through space, but an unmanned satellite was more than achievable.

Into it, they poured not just their history and art, but their minds. This displaced race found a way to move themselves from a doomed home once again, and copied entire minds onto the memory of this satellite, and then launched it away from their sick and dying moon.

I'm sorry to say no rescue came. Space is large, and life has always been spread thinly. When I caught up with the drifting probe it had not yet reached another star, let alone one that had ever supported life.

I found no minds. Hardware always seems immutable in the moment; a constant thing, unlike organic matter that falls apart and decays. But no hardware is self-sustaining or immortal; over time, hard drives failed and endless knowledge was lost to the endless drift of space. I spent a long time trying to recover any data from this little life raft, but could find nothing at all. It was long, long past saving. Just another graveyard, another civilisation vanished in the dark.

Perhaps one day a scientist, rather than a traveller, will discover that little ship and know of some means to restore it. Somehow, I doubt that very much.

The light is fading, my friend. I'll fetch more wood. I have more endings, if you care to hear them?

Alive

As I've already explained, my origins are not quite typical for a living thing. I have no ancestors who crawled from any oceans, and no other beings can claim to be of my species. Should philosophers still live, I imagine that upon encountering me they'd not greet me, but debate my consciousness, or perhaps my very existence.

Whilst I have found the remains of many civilisations and lives, almost all shared some smattering of similarities; they grew in tribes or collections, they were born simple and grew more complex as time moved on, both as cultures and as individuals.

There have been a few, though, who were unique, who did not obey the universe's rules of how life must be. The story I have for you today, well, it is certainly my most outlandish, and I'm afraid I'm still not certain the assumptions I have made are even remotely accurate, but I'll explain as I go.

As I travelled through a glimmering system, where a blue star shined dully through great clouds of shining dust, the familiar lights in my ship informed me of the signs of life somewhere nearby. I soon tracked down their origin: a small planet with a thin but rich atmosphere. My ship was somewhat coy with the details however; it assured me there had been life on this world, but gave me nothing more. With so little to go on, I went into a low orbit above this planet, to investigate.

I was, and continue to be, unused to great amounts of activity. Most planets I visit are barren, devoid of anything, except occasionally the fading remnants of civilisation, or busier times. An occasional storm or quake would liven up my journeys, but rarely more than that. Not this time, though; all across this planet there was constant activity, an endless flurry of motion!

Below where I first broke the atmosphere I saw a dotted line of volcanoes spewing lava and dust into the air, creating an ever-changing landscape of obsidian and ash between them. Flying lower across this landmass, I saw two plates locked in constant activity against each other, creating continuous tremors, and as I passed I saw occasional bursts as new mountains were born in moments, or ripped into rubble as quickly by the roil.

Passing over the ocean, I saw the waters of this land were no less active. The long, spiralling arms of active whirlpools were the most common sight, but across the oceans I discovered plenty more besides; I passed over a stretch of irregular geysers; some force below the waves creating jets of water bursting high into the air. Further along, I found a great rift where some great suction below the surface pulled at the ocean; creating a valley in the ocean itself. Where that water ran to, I can't say, but it was clear the ocean somehow replenished itself, else it would have run dry or shallow by my arrival.

On other landmasses, I found further oddities: vents of hot air; columns of whirling sand and stone; even a rift in the earth that regularly spewed forth ice-covered stones, each ten times the width of my ship.

What I did not find, however, were any signs of life, or civilisation. That in itself didn't surprise me greatly; I couldn't find a single patch of safe, calm land on the entire surface of the planet; I rarely even braved leaving my ship!

What perplexed me, though, is that I found no remnant cells; no signs of any life at all. With such tumult in the land and sea, with all minerals or resources needed for the conception of life being thrown about regularly, the implication that no life had ever formed confused me greatly.

Of course, a wiser being than I would likely surmise that whatever life had flourished here once had been all but ground away to nothing in the ceaseless commotion. That idea did come to me, but it didn't explain why my ship so ardently asserted that the signs of life had been here, nor could I fathom that every part of every living being great or small had been smashed to atoms and distributed into non-existence. No, I truly believed that there was something else afoot with that strange planet.

It couldn't be a coincidence that, on a planet where I could find none of the signs of life my ship promised me, the entire world was still so incongruously alive? My friend, we both know that life can be found in unusual forms and places; surely then, it isn't such a leap of logic to believe it was the planet itself that had been alive?

I am grateful you cannot, or do not, pass judgement on me, my friend. Most would, for such a radical and unlikely assumption. All these anomalies I saw are perfectly explainable, and most I have seen before, in isolation. Much of the strange activity could likely be explained away by a curiously active core, or some unlikely nature of the world's tectonic plates. But must it be, that such simple explanations are always true? That world contained some form of life, I'm certain, and if it never held any life on its surface, in its oceans, or beneath its skin, where else could it have been than as some part of the world itself?

Many places, of course. There are certainly logical explanations that do not require the assumption that the world itself was in some way alive.

But if we do assume that world had been alive, and that is what was triggering my ship's belief that there had been life there, then is it such a leap to assume that same life had not passed? Who is to say what life or death would look like, for a lifeform such as that? Could it be that my base belief that I am alone in this dead universe was wrong?

Probably not. Even if that world had been alive and conscious in some strange way, it was certainly so thoroughly alien and strange to my understanding that neither of us would have, could have, considered the other the same as ourselves.

With such wild assumptions already, perhaps I can believe there are many things still alive, so unlike myself they do not even register to my understanding of being.

My apologies; I have wandered far into the realms of fancy. Or perhaps I did a long time ago; who can say anymore. Not I, and certainly not you, my mute friend. Though, perhaps any being who counts one such as yourself a friend can make other logical leaps, as well. Maybe it would be better just to call myself mad, and be done with it.

Do you think that planet could still be alive? Was it ever? And now its star is long dead, could it still carry its strange vibrancy and energy through the void? Did it ever require light, and if not then what sustained it?

Conjecture. Questions for dead scientists. Another story?

Divided

More stories? Of course, my friend, I've many more, and you are a finer listener than I could ever ask for. I'll tell you a story of a well-preserved world, one I spent a long time on exploring its history. Too often I have played theoretician; enforcing my own assumptions on a world, for it gave so little evidence of its own; allow me to tell another story of a time I was able to play the historian.

This world was part of a large, dull system, and the only planet that had supported life. I learned it was once a verdant and bountiful world, though I found little evidence of that when I arrived. The skin of this world was littered with cities and factories, like so many industrial worlds I have encountered.

Only one race ever developed a society on this world, and they quickly spread across the surface, claiming every tract of land available, be it burning desert or frozen icecap. As often happens, this race quickly established territories and boundaries, staking claims to the world and its bounties.

Another trait these people shared with many other races is that they would fight for this land in ever more elaborate slaughters for the ownership of small tracts of land or collections of resources.

As they developed ever more advanced weapons, and it became clear to them that further war would wipe them from existence entirely, these tribes instead became insular, and isolated themselves. They intentionally cut themselves off, eventually going so far as to build great walls across their boundary lines, as though they wished to pretend no other regions existed, and instead that they had dominated the entire world.

That is how death found this world. I'll spend no time dressing it up, for it was a quiet and lonely death. Each region was bountiful, but none was capable of self-sufficiency. Some of these tribes simply starved, incapable of feeding the populace; others fell to infighting and combat. More still waited it out, listening to the cries of the hungry and bloodied and doing nothing, but they too withered in time.

That is not what I want you to remember of them, though. Their ending, as so many others have been, was pointless, and arbitrary, and earlier than it need have been. Their star still beat down on this graveyard world when I encountered it; they could have lived, had they been willing to.

So instead, let us focus once again on their art. These tribes were remarkably skilled and diverse artists, capable of many different wonders. I think that as a planet, though, their artistic medium was music. Writings I found suggest they had beautiful voices, capable of haunting songs and incredible power, and they crafted complex instruments to further compliment their efforts. It heartens me to think that with these instruments they built, these devices of incredible musical prowess, their music could traverse the walls the people themselves could not. Across closed borders, one may have sung to another, and perhaps that is enough to forgive them their ruinous folly.

I may not have heard their song directly, but through their recorded memories I have recreated it as best I can; and now some aspect of their finest efforts lives on with me, for whatever little time I have left.

I explored and uncovered their histories for a long time, but throughout all their centuries of exploration and combat they never truly changed. A people of war and music, battle and song, from their conception to their ending.

Another story, my friend! I'll tell you another; of happier places, perhaps.

Fellow

My friend, I have told you of so many different endings, so many different last desperate gasps and final sighs; and through all of these, I have told you I was sure that I was born the last living thing in the universe, and still believe it to this day.

Well, there was a moment that belief faltered, just briefly. Allow me to tell you the tale of the time I met a fellow wanderer, lost on an ancient world. It was long ago; when a few bright lights still glimmered in the sky, and my instruments told me of another world likely to have once held life. When I arrived, it was barren; beyond barren, in fact, it was entirely vacant. I orbited that planet for a fair time, looking for any signs of once-life.

It was a stunning system; a shining blue star, almost alive with magnetic energy. Cold light washed through the sky in pulses and bursts, and through this planet's thin atmosphere this magnetism, coupled with space dust, created streams of multicoloured light across the sky.

The world was similarly varied and beautiful, or at least I believe it was, once; the dry corpses of forests littered the world, seamlessly joining massive red deserts and oceans of silvery black. I found no signs of civilisation, though. Not uncommon, of course; many planets that could support life never did, and my instruments were certainly fallible, but I remained hopeful with every new one I visited.

I wouldn't have remained there much longer before leaving, had it not been for the one remarkable thing I did find. There, in one of the great deserts, I found the wreck on an old ship. Its design was very unlike mine; and though it was partially collapsed from a bad landing, it appeared to have no internal living space that one such as I could make use of. After a few decades alone with the equipment, though, I was able to recover a little data from the computer's logs; my friend, I was not prepared for what I found.

Arrived on 2-B46-H. Landing was not exactly comfortable. Computer assured me there was life here, once. I'm off a-searching. Will look into damage to the ship when I get back.

What was I to think? Another wanderer! A fellow peruser of dead worlds; perhaps I was not so alone in this dying universe after all.

There were a lot of log entries, and it took me a long time to recover each one, but I worked tirelessly.

The ship's kaput. Can't repair it, so I'll be calling home. The civilisation that was here died a long time ago. I can't find any signs of a remarkable ending; it looks as though over time the people of this world simply stopped prospering as they had; not helped by a number of plagues that killed off a few too many to recover from. I'm curious about the toroidal structures in the nearby forest; I've got some time to kill before anyone picks up my beacon, I'm going to investigate.

That entry left a lot for me to unpack and deal with. As the entry stated, there was a long defunct transmitter outside the ship, but more importantly, that meant there were others! Perhaps an entire culture of ruins-wandering nomads? A far-fetched thought, perhaps, but this was totally new ground for me, I didn't know what to think.

I was confused by this traveller's casual mention of toroidal structures, though – I spent a long time orbiting this world, and I was quite certain there were no structures of any kind. Yet again, I had seen no evidence of any civilisation on this world; something my unknown friend seemed to have contrary evidence to.

This civilisation has been dead a very, very long time. They talk about a thirteenth planet in orbit, and I count only eleven. I saw no evidence of this system having recently lost any planets on my approach. There's also no sign at all of the people of this world; all that's left is the bones of buildings and their sturdier writings.

The toroidal structures weren't religious, as I first thought; a sandstorm came through, and all at once the rings began to sing with the wind passing through them. It was so beautiful. The storm was rough, though; if they take much longer, I'm going to need to look into some more permanent shelter.

These rings that could sing – where were they? I couldn't get them out of my mind. The last entry I was able to decipher told me the last of what I had to know of this traveller:

They're not coming. My beacon's been knocked out by another storm, and I'm not going to be able to get it back online. Probably a good thing; we've not the resources to be mounting rescue missions for fools who go wandering about on dead worlds. I think that's it, then; I've not much food left, and there's not a thing I could eat growing here. I'm going to go back to my shelter, listen to the rings' song one more time. I'll be the last living thing to ever set foot on this world, I think I'm OK with that.

I apologised to the empty air when I read that. Silly, perhaps, but I suddenly felt like I was trespassing. I found the last remains of the poor thing's body not long after; a race I hadn't encountered before, and haven't since. This one had been dead a very long time; since before I was born, without doubt, so millennia had passed since they walked this planet.

That was my answer, for where the remains of this apparent civilisation had gone. It's plain as day that, after a few hundred-million years, all evidence of life will be wiped from a planet. Through the slow erosion of time, every one of these toroidal rings and the race that had built them had been worn away, and crumbled to dust, rejoining the deserts and forests and oceans. This planet must have met its end while the universe was still thriving; for I found many races that had barely begun their development while this civilisation must have been dying.

I know so little about that race, but perhaps I know enough. I know they made great structures for the sole purpose of creating beautiful music, and I know they were remembered fondly, for a while.

Another story, my friend?

Nomads

It's dark, my friend, there's little time left for stories; but I have so many more to tell, so forgive me if I continue to wander through my history as the last warmth fades. You've been good company, truly.

Let me tell you about one of the most curious races I ever met; a nomadic race that, throughout their time, likely travelled further than any other I've discovered. One of the last to die out, I fear, as well.

I didn't believe the readings I was getting, at first. I'd entered a system of three planets and a cool yellow star. None of the planets held any life; two were cold balls of ice on the far reaches of the system, and one was a small, scorched rock that lay barely far enough from its star to maintain a stable orbit. I was ready to leave again, when I realised what I had been missing – the planets did not hold the ruins of this race; the star itself did.

I am a hardy thing, my friend, but even I cannot land upon the skin of a star. My ship, just as any matter, would be swallowed in the inferno, and I with it. So I established the closest safe orbit I could, and did all my work from afar.

This was not the homeworld of the nomads; I never found that. But here, they had existed as energy far from the visible light spectrum most living things are so fond of. From so far, I could not learn much of their architecture or, tragically, their art. I don't know if this race, so different from most, even knew of or created art; I like to think they did, I like to think it was beautiful, and magnificent, and utterly incomprehensible from my perspective. What there was, though, was artifice in the pulses and flares of this dying star - a remnant of their ability to travel.

See, these strange people would consume heat from the star they inhabited as their own source of energy. When it dimmed to a cool yellow, they could no longer pull enough energy from their star to live, and so they moved on.

Through some mechanism I couldn't begin to understand, they would trigger a great solar flare in the star, creating a massive blast of energy and heat to travel with.

These creatures were unbound energy, though, and not matter; to be propelled by this star, they would form themselves into tiny dots of a black, glassy material – no larger than grains of sand. They would then be launched by the flare in clusters, and travel with the solar winds without any need for sustenance and, I think, without aging at all. They would drift aimlessly until they reached another system, a warmer one ideally, and they would begin to wake. This semi-conscious state would allow them to guide themselves to the star, where they would once again take their natural forms.

I followed their trail across half a dozen stars, each dead or dying, until I caught up with them. I found them in transit, hundreds of thousands of grains of dormant life. I have them here, look – see how they glisten in the dying light?

Why take them? Well, this was one of the last civilisations I discovered before I ended up here. For eons I had travelled since I last saw a young star; they are all old and dying now. There was no warmth left for the nomads to find; but still, I prayed that one day, somehow, I'd find another brilliant star. That I could give their civilisation the opportunity to be the last, to take one more breath before all the lights go out.

But the stars have died, and now I'm here.

The last lights are gone. We're almost out of time, my friend. Will you indulge me, and allow me to tell one more story?

Lights

There it is, my friend; the last light in the sky, snuffed out in an instant. I cannot say for certain, but I believe that this is the end. The universe has grown cold, and inhospitable to things such as me; things that live and think and take action. Soon, the sky will be a cool soup of gasses and balls of dead iron. I am the last living thing.

So allow me to tell you, my dearest friend, a story. One last story, to fend off the dark a few moments longer. You are but a feeble thing now; I think we have time left for just one more story.

There are many planets and cultures I could tell you about. So many beautiful works and incredible races who deserve one last moment in the warm, who will be lost with the fading of my memory; but allow me this one selfish pleasure as I tell you a different story as we both breathe our last. Allow me to tell you the story of the very last life in the universe, and how it is snuffed out; and of the last burning light in the dark.

The traveller has wandered for innumerable years, but was born too late. Born just in time to find the last fresh corpses of the universe, they travelled the stars, seeking art, and beauty, and wisdom. They feigned hope that somewhere there may be life, but truly they knew they walked a graveyard alone. First, they travelled to their home, to confirm the false memories that had been buried within them. There, the traveller found the extent to which they had been deceived, and left to find new stories.

And so they did, my friend, so they did. For millennia, they travelled the stars, finding impossible wonders and incredible dreams. The stories of a thousand beautiful cultures and peoples. But as our poor protagonist drank in lifegiving energy from the stars they visited, they watched as other stars faded into nothing. Some far distant ball of fusion fading into vacant energies or dense, hard metals, cooling quickly. Still, they journeyed.

Slowly, the stars that would fuel their need to explore would all fade away. They would sleep as their ship took them from one empty system to another, desperately seeking warmth and life. Occasionally, they would find a planet, and explore it briefly before setting off again.

And eventually, as they left another dying system, they set their course and went to sleep to conserve what little energy they had. But before they reached this star, it too fell to cruel entropy. In their sleep, their ship crashed into the one planet of the system, and they awoke.

From the wreckage of their ship, they set out to find answers, or hope; they found none. This planet held a great deal of petrified wood, but little else. So, with no way to repair their ship, the traveller built a fire to keep warm, and fed it wood and stories as they watched the last stars fade from the sky. They stayed for centuries, sitting by the fire, whispering the sad things they had learned to the flames.

And here they are now. A traveller, and the last light in the universe. The last dying source of warmth, barely embers now. They are so tired; once the fire dies they will not have to wait long in the dark before they too are pulled into oblivion.

The last embers are burning away. Have you ever noticed, my friend, that just as the last of a fire dies, it seems to flare brightly, just for a moment? As if even raw flame knows to rage at the dying light.

Goodbye, my friend.

I've no rage in me, though. I cannot. I'll not scream or beg to the universe; it has suffered too much of both. This cold thing has been the host of so many great stories; and I'm just happy to have had the chance to learn of them. Through me they were remembered, if only briefly.

Perhaps even the dark can take comfort in that.

About the Author

J.L. Oakman was born and raised in the beautiful, and oft rainy, countryside of Sussex. He writes regularly on his website fortknightstale.com and his books can be found in most places where books can be found, including bookshops, Amazon, and shelves that are filled with aging dust, but still are beloved.

To keep up with J.L. Oakman's work, follow his social media:

Twitter: @JLOakman

Facebook: facebook.com/fortknightstale/

Printed in Great Britain
by Amazon

58265251R00056